U

THOMAS MORE

A Phoenix Paperback

First published in Everyman in 1994

J. M. Dent
A division of Orion Books Ltd
Orion House, 5 Upper St Martin's Lane, London WC2H 9EA

This abridged edition, published in 1996 by Phoenix,
contains pages 55 to 97 of The Second Book of Utopia,
from *Utopia* by Thomas More.

Cover illustration: Portrait of Sir Thomas More by Hans Holbein,
(1497/8–1543), © Frick Collection, New York/Bridgeman Art Library

ISBN 1 85799 527 9

Typeset by CentraCet Ltd, Cambridge
Printed in Great Britain by
Clays Ltd, St Ives plc

The Communication of
Raphael Hythloday

Concerning the beststate of a commonwealth containing the description of Utopia, with a large declaration of the politic government and of all the good laws and orders of the same land.

The island of Utopia containeth in breadth in the middle part of it (for there it is broadest) 200 miles. Which breadth continueth through the most part of the land, saving that by little and little it cometh in and waxeth narrower towards both the ends. Which fetching about a circuit or compass of 500 miles, do fashion the whole island like to the new moon. Between these two corners the sea runneth in, dividing them asunder by the distance of eleven miles or thereabouts, and there surmounteth into a large and wide sea, which by reason that the land on every side compasseth it about and sheltereth it from the winds, is not rough nor mounteth not with great waves, but almost floweth quietly, not much unlike a great standing pool, and maketh wellnigh all the space within the belly of the land in manner of a haven, and to the great commodity of the inhabitants receiveth in ships towards every part of the land. The forefronts or frontiers of the two corners, what with fords and shelves and what with rocks, be very jeopardous and dangerous. In the middle distance between them both standeth up above the water a great rock, which therefore is nothing perilous because it is in sight. Upon the top of this rock is a fair and a strong tower builded, which they hold with a garrison of men. Other rocks there be lying hid under the water, which therefore be dangerous. The channels be known only to themselves, and therefore it seldom chanceth that any stranger unless be he guided by an Utopian, can come into this haven, insomuch that they themselves could scarcely enter without jeopardy, but that their way is directed and ruled by certain landmarks standing on the shore. By turning, translating, and removing these marks into other places they may destroy their enemies' navies, be they never so many. The outside or utter circuit of the land is also full of havens, but the landing is so surely fenced, what by nature and what by workmanship of man's hand, that a few defenders may drive back many armies.

Howbeit, as they say and as the fashion of the place itself doth partly shew, it was not ever compassed about with the sea. But King Utopus, whose name as conqueror the island beareth (for before his time it was called Abraxa), which also brought the rude and wild people to that excellent perfection in all good fashions, humanity, and civil gentleness, wherein they now go beyond all the people of the world, even at his first arriving and entering upon the land, forthwith obtaining the victory, caused fifteen miles space of uplandish ground, where the sea had no passage, to be cut and digged up, and so brought the sea round about the land. He set to this work not only the inhabitants of the island (because they should not think it done in contumely and despite) but also all his own soldiers. Thus the work, being divided into so great a number of workmen, was with exceeding marvellous speed dispatched. Insomuch that the borderers, which at the first began to mock and to jest at this vain enterprise, then turned their derision to marvel at the success and to fear. There be in the island fifty-four large and fair cities, or shire towns, agreeing all together in one tongue, in like manners, institutions, and laws. They be all set and situate alike, and in all points fashioned alike, as far forth as the place or plot suffereth.

Of these cities they that be nighest together be twenty-four miles asunder. Again, there is none of them distant from the next above one day's journey afoot. There come yearly to Amaurote out of every city three old men wise and well experienced, there to entreat and debate of the common matters of the land. For this city (because it standeth just in the midst of the island, and is therefore most meet for the ambassadors of all parts of the realm) is taken for the chief and head city. The precincts and bounds of the shires be so commodiously appointed out and set forth for the cities, that none of them all hath of any side less than twenty miles of ground, and of some side also much more, as of that part where the cities be of farther distance asunder. None of the cities desire to enlarge the bounds and limits of their shires, for they count themselves rather the good husbands than the owners of their lands.

They have in the country, in all parts of the shire, houses or farms builded, well appointed and furnished with all sorts of instruments and tools belonging to husbandry. These houses be inhabited of the citizens which come thither to dwell by course. No household or farm in the country hath fewer than forty persons, men and women, besides two bondmen which be all under the rule and order of the goodman and the goodwife of the house, being both very sage, discreet, and ancient persons. And every thirty farms or families have one head ruler which is called a Philarch, being as it were a head bailiff. Out of every one of these families or farms cometh every year into the city twenty persons which have continued two years before in the country. In their place so many fresh be sent thither out of the city, who, of them that have been there a year already and be therefore expert and cunning in husbandry, shall be instructed and taught. And they the next year shall teach other. This order is used for fear that either scarceness of victuals or some other like incommodity should chance, through lack of knowledge if they should be altogether new and fresh and unexpert in husbandry. This manner and fashion of yearly changing and renewing the occupiers of husbandry, though it be solemn and customably used to the intent that no man shall be constrained against his will to continue long in that hard and sharp kind of life, yet many of them have such a pleasure and delight in husbandry that they obtain a longer space of years. These husbandmen plow and till the ground, and breed up cattle, and provide and make ready wood which they carry to the city either by land or by water as they may most conveniently. They bring up a great multitude of pullen, and that by a marvellous policy. For the hens do not sit upon the eggs, but by keeping them in a certain equal heat they bring life into them and hatch them. The chickens, as soon as they be come out of the shell, follow men and women instead of the hens. They bring up very few horses, nor none but very fierce ones; and that for none other use or purpose, but only to exercise their youth in riding and feats of arms, for oxen be put to all the labour of plowing and drawing. Which they grant to be not so good as horses at a sudden brunt and (as we say) at a dead lift, but yet they hold opinion that oxen will abide and suffer much more labour, pain, and hardness than horses will. And they think that oxen be not in danger and subject unto so many diseases, and that they be kept and maintained with much less cost and charge, and finally that they be good for meat when they be past labour. They sow corn only for bread, for their drink is either wine made of grapes or else of apples or pears, or else it is clear water, and many times mead made of honey or liquorice sodden in water, for thereof they have great store. And though they know certainly (for they know it perfectly indeed) how much victuals the city with the whole country or shire round about it doth spend, yet they sow much more corn and breed up much more cattle than serveth for their own use, parting the overplus among their borderers. Whatsoever necessary things be lacking in the country, all such stuff they fetch out of the city where without any exchange they easily obtain it of the magistrates of the city. For every month many of them go into the city on the holy day. When their harvest day draweth near and is at hand, then the Philarchs, which be the head officers and bailiffs of husbandry, send word to the magistrates of the city what number of harvest men is needful to be sent to them out of the city. The which company of harvest men being ready at the day appointed, almost in one fair day dispatcheth all the harvest work.

Of the cities and namely of Amaurote

As for their cities, whoso knoweth one of them knoweth them all, they be all so like one to another as far forth as the nature of the place permitteth. I will describe, therefore, to you one or other of them, for it skilleth not greatly which, but which rather than Amaurote? Of them all this is the worthiest and of most dignity. For the residue knowledge it for the head city because there is the council house. Nor to me any of them all is better beloved, as wherein I lived five whole years together. The city of Amaurote standeth upon the side of a low hill, in fashion almost four-square. For the breadth of it beginneth a little beneath the top of the hill, and still continueth by the space of two miles until it come to the river of Anyder. The length of it, which lieth by the river's side, is somewhat more. The river of Anyder riseth four and twenty miles above Amaurote out of a little spring, but being increased by other small rivers and brooks that run into it, and among other two somewhat big ones, before the city it is half a mile broad, and farther broader. And forty miles beyond the city it falleth into the ocean sea. By all that space that lieth between the sea and the city, and certain miles also above the city, the water ebbeth and floweth six hours together with a swift tide. When the sea floweth in, for the length of thirty miles it filleth all the Anyder with salt water, and driveth back the fresh water of the river. And somewhat farther it changeth the sweetness of the fresh water with saltness. But a little beyond that the river waxeth sweet, and runneth forby the city fresh and pleasant. And when the sea ebbeth and goeth back again, the fresh water followeth it almost even to the very fall into the sea. There goeth a bridge over the river, made not of piles or of timber, but of stonework with gorgeous and substantial arches at that part of the city that is farthest from the sea, to the intent 7 that ships may pass along forby all the side of the city without let. They have also another river which, indeed, is not very great, but it runneth gently and pleasantly. For it riseth even out of the same hill that the city standeth upon, and runneth down a slope through the midst of the city into Anyder. And because it riseth a little without the city, the Amaurotians have enclosed the head spring of it with strong fences and bulwarks, and so have joined it to the city. This is done to the intent that the water should not be stopped nor turned away or poisoned if their enemies should chance to come upon them. From thence the water is derived and conveyed down in channels of brick divers ways into the lower parts of the city. Where that cannot be done, by reason that the place will not suffer it, there they gather the rain water in great cisterns, which doeth them as good service.

The city is compassed about with a high and thick stone wall full of turrets and bulwarks. A dry ditch, but deep and broad and overgrown with bushes, briars, and thorns, goeth about three sides or quarters of the city. To the fourth side the river itself serveth for a ditch. The streets be appointed and set forth very commodious and handsome, both for carriage and also against the winds. The houses be of fair and gorgeous building, and on the street side they stand joined together in a long row through the whole street without any partition or separation. The streets be twenty foot broad. On the back side of the houses, through the whole length of the street, lie large gardens enclosed round about with the back part of the streets. Every house hath two doors, one into the street, and a postern door on the back side into the garden. These doors be made with two leaves never locked nor bolted, so easy to be opened, that they will follow the least drawing of a finger, and shut again alone. Whoso will may go in, for there is nothing within the houses that is private or any man's own. And every tenth year they change their houses by lot.

They set great store by their gardens. In them they have vineyards, all manner of fruit, herbs, and flowers, so pleasant, so well furnished, and so finely kept, that I never saw thing more fruitful nor better trimmed in any place. Their study and diligence herein cometh not only of pleasure, but also of a certain strife and contention that is between street and street concerning the trimming, husbanding, and furnishing of their gardens, every man for his own part. And verily you shall not lightly find in all the city anything that is more commodious, either for the profit of the citizens or for pleasure. And therefore it may seem that the first founder of the city minded nothing so much as these gardens. For they say that King Utopus himself, even at the first beginning, appointed and drew forth the platform of the city into this fashion and figure that it hath now, but the gallant garnishing and the beautiful setting forth of it, whereunto he saw that one man's age would not suffice, that he left to his posterity. For their chronicles, which they keep written with all 9 diligent circumspection, containing the history of 1760 years, even from the first conquest of the island, record and witness that the houses in the beginning were very low and like homely cottages or poor shepherd houses, made, at all adventures, of every rude piece of timber that came first to hand, with mud walls and ridged roofs thatched over with straw. But now the houses be curiously builded after a gorgeous and gallant sort, with three storeys one over another. The outsides of the walls be made either of hard flint or of plaster, or else of brick, and the inner sides be well strengthened with timber work. The roofs be plain and flat, covered with a certain kind of plaster that is of no cost, and yet so tempered that no fire can hurt or perish it, and withstandeth the violence of the weather better than any lead. They keep the wind out of their windows with glass, for it is there much used, and somewhere also with fine linen cloth dipped in oil or amber, and that for two commodities, for by this means more light cometh in, and the wind is better kept out.

Of the Magistrates

Every thirty families or farms choose them yearly an officer which in their old language is called the Syphogrant, and by a newer name the Philarch. Every ten Syphogrants, with all their thirty families, be under an officer which was once called the Tranibore, now the chief Philarch. Moreover, as concerning the election of the prince, all the Syphogrants, which be in number 200, first be sworn to choose him whom they think most meet and expedient. Then by a secret election they name prince one of those four whom the people before named unto them. For out of the four quarters of the city there be four chosen, out of every quarter one, to stand for the election, which be put up to the council. The prince's office continueth all his lifetime, unless he be deposed or put down for suspicion of tyranny. They choose the Tranibores yearly, but lightly they change them not. All the other officers be but for one year. The Tranibores every third day, and sometimes, if need be, oftener, come into the council house with the prince. Their counsel is concerning the commonwealth. If there be any controversies among the commoners, which be very few, they dispatch and end them by and by. They take ever two Syphogrants to them in council, and every day a new couple. And it is provided that nothing touching the commonwealth shall be confirmed and ratified unless it have been reasoned of and debated three days in the council before it be decreed. It is death to have any consultation for the commonwealth out of the council or the place of the common election. This statute, they say, was made to the intent that the prince and Tranibores might not easily conspire together to oppress the people by tyranny, and to change the state of the weal-public. Therefore matters of great weight and importance be brought to the election house of the Syphogrants, which open the matter to their families and afterward, when they have consulted among themselves, they show their device to the council. Sometimes the matter is brought before the council of the whole island. Furthermore, this custom also the council useth, to dispute or reason of no matter the same day that it is first proposed or put forth, but to defer it to the next sitting of the council. Because that no man, when he hath rashly there spoken that cometh to his tongue's end, shall then afterward rather study for reasons wherewith to defend and maintain his first foolish sentence, than for the commodity of the commonwealth, as one rather willing the harm or hindrance of the weal-public than any loss or diminution of his own existimation, and as one that would be ashamed (which is a very foolish shame) to be counted anything at the first overseen in the matter. Who at the first ought to have spoken rather wisely than hastily or rashly.

Of Sciences, Crafts, and Occupations

Husbandry is a science common to them all in general, both men and women, wherein they be all expert and cunning. In this they be all instructed even from their youth, partly in their schools with traditions and precepts, and partly in the country nigh the city, brought up, as it were in playing, not only beholding the use of it, but by occasion of exercising their bodies practising it also.

Besides husbandry, which (as I said) is common to them all, every one of them learneth one or other several and particular science as his own proper craft. That is most commonly either clothworking in wool or flax, or masonry, or the smith's craft, or the carpenter's science. For there is none other occupation that any number to speak of doth use there. For their garments, which throughout all the island be of one fashion (saving that there is a difference between the man's garment and the woman's, between the married and the unmarried), and this one continueth for evermore unchanged, seemly and comely to the eye, no let to the moving and wielding of the body, also fit both for winter and summer. As for these garments (I say) every family maketh their own. But of the other foresaid crafts every man learneth one, and not only the men, but also the women. But the women, as the weaker sort, be put to the easier crafts, as to work wool and flax; the more laboursome sciences be committed to the men. For the most part every man is brought up in his father's craft, for most commonly they be naturally thereto bent and inclined. But if a man's mind stand to any other, he is by adoption put into a family of that occupation which he doth most fantasy. Whom not only his father but also the magistrates do diligently look to that he be put to a discreet and an honest householder. Yea, and if any person when he hath learned one craft be desirous to learn also another, he is likewise suffered and permitted. When he hath learned both, he occupieth whether he will, unless the city have more need of the one than of the other.

The chief and almost the only office of the Syphogrants is to see and take heed that no man sit idle, but that every one apply his own craft with earnest diligence; and yet for all that, not to be wearied from early in the morning to late in the evening with continual work, like labouring and toiling beasts. For this is worse than the miserable and wretched condition of bondmen, which nevertheless is almost everywhere the life of workmen and artificers, saving in Utopia. For they, dividing the day and the night into twenty-four just hours, appoint and assign only six of those hours to work before noon, upon the which they go straight to dinner. And after dinner, when they have rested two hours, then they work three hours, and upon that they go to supper. About eight of the clock in the evening (counting one of the clock at the first hour after noon) they go to bed; eight hours they give to sleep. All the void time that is between the hours of work, sleep, and meat, that they be suffered to bestow, every man as he liketh best himself. Not to the intent that they should misspend this time in riot or slothfulness, but being then licensed from the labour of their own occupations, to bestow the time well and thriftily upon some other science as shall please them. For it is a solemn custom there, to have lectures daily early in the morning, where to be present they only be constrained that be namely chosen and appointed to learning. Howbeit, a great multitude of every sort of people, both men and women, go to hear lectures, some one and some another, as every man's nature is inclined. Yet, this notwithstanding, if any man had rather bestow this time upon his own occupation (as it chanceth in many whose minds rise not in the contemplation of any science liberal), he is not letted nor prohibited, but is also praised and commended as profitable to the commonwealth. After supper they bestow one hour in play, in summer in their gardens, in winter in their common halls where they dine and sup. There they exercise themselves in music, or else in honest and wholesome communication. Dice-play and such other foolish and pernicious games they know not; but they use two games not much unlike the chess. The one is the battle of numbers, wherein one number stealeth away another. The other is wherein vices fight with virtues, as it were in battle array or a set field. In the which game is very properly shewed both the strife and discord that vices have among themselves, and again their unity and concord against virtues; and also what vices be repugnant to what virtues; with what power and strength they assail them openly; by what wiles and subtlety they assault them secretly; with what help and aid the virtues resist and overcome the puissance of the vices; by what craft they frustrate their purposes; and, finally, by what sleight or means the one getteth the victory.

But here lest you be deceived, one thing you must look more narrowly upon. For seeing they bestow but six hours in work, perchance you may think that the lack of some necessary things hereof may ensue. But this is nothing so. For that small time is not only enough but also too much for the store and abundance of all things that be requisite either for the necessity or commodity of life. The which thing you also shall perceive if you weigh and consider with yourselves how great a part of the people in other countries liveth idle. First, almost all women, which be the half of the whole number, or else, if the women be somewhere occupied, there most commonly in their stead the men be idle. Besides this, how great and how idle a company is there of priests and religious men, as they call them! Put thereto all rich men, specially all landed men, which commonly be called gentlemen and noblemen. Take into this number also their servants, I mean all that flock of stout bragging rushbucklers; join to them also sturdy and valiant beggars, cloaking their idle life under the colour of some disease or sickness, and truly you shall find them much fewer than you thought, by whose labour all these things are wrought that in men's affairs are now daily used and frequented. Now consider with yourself of these few that do work, how few be occupied in necessary works. For where money beareth all the swing, there many vain and superfluous occupations must needs be used, to serve only for riotous superfluity and unhonest pleasure. For the same multitude that now is occupied in work, if they were divided into so few occupations as the necessary use of nature requireth, in so great plenty of things as then of necessity would ensue doubtless the prices would be too little for the artificers to maintain their livings. But if all these that be now busied about unprofitable occupations, with all the whole flock of them that live idly and slothfully, which consume and waste every one of them more of these things that come by other men's labour than two of the workmen themselves do, if all these (I say) were set to profitable occupations, you easily perceive how little time would be enough, yea, and too much, to store us with all things that may be requisite either for necessity or for commodity, yea, or for pleasure, so that the same pleasure be true and natural.

And this in Utopia the thing itself maketh manifest and plain. For there, in all the city with the whole country or shire adjoining to it, scarcely 500 persons of all the whole number of men and women that be neither too old nor too weak to work be licensed and discharged from labour. Among them be the Syphogrants, who, though they be by the laws exempt and privileged from labour, yet they exempt not themselves, to the intent that they may the rather by their example provoke others to work. The same vacation from labour do they also enjoy to whom the people, persuaded by the commendation of the priests and secret election of the Syphogrants, have given a perpetual licence from labour to learning. But if any one of them prove not according to the expectation and hope of him conceived, he is forthwith plucked back to the company of artificers. And contrariwise, often it chanceth that a handicraftsman doth so earnestly bestow his vacant amd spare hours in learning, and through diligence so profiteth therein, that he is taken from his handy occupation and promoted to the company of the learned. Out of this order of the learned be chosen ambassadors, priests, Tranibores, and finally the prince himself, whom they in their old tongue call Barzanes and, by a newer name, Adamus. The residue of the people being neither idle nor yet occupied about unprofitable exercises, it may be easily judged in how few hours how much good work by them may be done and dispatched towards those things that I have spoken of.

This commodity they have also above other, that in the most part of necessary occupations they need not so much work as other nations do. For, first of all, the building or repairing of houses asketh everywhere so many men's continual labour, because that the unthrifty here suffereth the houses that his father builded in continuance of time to fall in decay. So that which he might have upholden with little cost, his successor is constrained to build it again anew, to his great charge. Yea, many times also the house that stood one man in much money, another is of so nice and so delicate a mind, that he setteth nothing by it; and, it being neglected and therefore shortly falling into ruin, be buildeth up another in another place with no less cost and charge. But among the Utopians, where all things be set in a good order and the commonwealth in a good stay, it very seldom chanceth that they choose a new plot to build an house upon. And they do not only find speedy and quick remedies for present faults, but also prevent them that be like to fall. And by this means their houses continue and last very long with little labour and small reparations; insomuch that this kind of workmen sometimes have almost nothing to do, but that they be commanded to hew timber at home, and to square and trim up stones, to the intent that if any work chance it may the speedlier rise.

Now, sir, in their apparel mark (I pray you) how few workmen they need. First of all, whiles they be at work they be covered homely with leather or skins that will last seven years. When they go forth abroad they cast upon them a cloak which hideth the other homely apparel. These cloaks throughout the whole island be all of one colour, and that is the natural colour of the wool. They therefore do not only spend much less woollen cloth than is spent in other countries, but also the same standeth them in much less cost. But linen cloth is made with less labour, and is therefore had more in use. But in linen cloth only whiteness, in woollen only cleanliness, is regarded. As for the smallness or fineness of the thread, that is nothing passed for. And this is the cause wherefore in other places four or five cloth gowns of divers colours and as many silk coats be not enough for one man. Yea, and if he be of the delicate and nice sort ten be too few, whereas there one garment will serve a man most commonly two years. For why should he desire more, seeing if he had them he should not be the better hapt or covered from cold, neither in his apparel any whit the comelier? Wherefore, seeing they be all exercised in profitable occupations, and that few artificers in the same crafts be sufficient, this is the cause that, plenty of all things being among them, they do sometimes bring forth an innumerable company of people to amend the highways if any be broken. Many times also, when they have no such work to be occupied about, an open proclamation is made that they shall bestow fewer hours in work. For the magistrates do not exercise their citizens against their wills in unneedful labours. For why, in the institution of that weal-public this end is only and chiefly pretended and minded, that what time may possibly be spared from the necessary occupations and affairs of the commonwealth, all that the citizens should withdraw from the bodily service to the free liberty of the mind and garnishing of the same. For herein they suppose the felicity of this life to consist.

Of their Living and Mutual Conversation together

But now will I declare how the citizens use themselves one towards another, what familiar occupying and entertainment there is among the people, and what fashion they use in the distribution of everything. First, the city consisteth of families; the families most commonly be made of kindreds. For the women, when they be married at a lawful age, they go into their husbands' houses, but the male children, with all the whole male offspring, continue still in their own family and be governed of the eldest and ancientest father, unless he dote for age, for then the next to him in age is placed in his room. But to the intent the prescript number of the citizens should neither decrease nor above measure increase, it is ordained that no family, which in every city be six thousand in the whole besides them of the country, shall at once have fewer children of the age of fourteen years or thereabout than ten or more the sixteen, for of children under this age no number can be prescribed or appointed. This measure or number is easily observed and kept by putting them that in fuller families be above the number into families of smaller increase. But if chance be that in the whole city the store increase above the just number, therewith they fill up the lack of other cities. But if so be that the multitude throughout the whole island pass and exceed the due number, then they choose out of every city certain citizens, and build up a town under their own laws in the next land where the inhabitants have much waste and unoccupied ground, receiving also of the same country people to them, if they will join and dwell with them. They thus joining and dwelling together do easily agree in one fashion of living, and that to the great wealth of both the peoples. For they so bring the matter about by their laws, that the ground which before was neither good nor profitable for the one nor for the other is now sufficient and fruitful enough for them both. But if the inhabitants of that land will not dwell with them to be ordered by their laws, then they drive them out of those bounds which they have limited and appointed out for themselves. And if they resist and rebel, then they make war against them. For they count this the most just cause of war, when any people holdeth a piece of ground void and vacant to no good nor profitable use, keeping others from the use and possession of it which notwithstanding by the law of nature ought thereof to be nourished and relieved. If any chance do so much diminish the number of any of their cities that it cannot be filled up again without the diminishing of the just number of the other cities (which they say chanced but twice since the beginning of the land through a great pestilent plague), then they fulfil and make up the number with citizens fetched out of their own foreign towns; for they had rather suffer their foreign towns to decay and perish than any city of their own island to be diminished.

But now again to the conversation of the citizens among themselves. The eldest (as I said) ruleth the family. The wives be ministers to their husbands, the children to their parents, and, to be short, the younger to their elders. Every city is divided into four equal parts or quarters. In the midst of every quarter there is a market-place of all manner of things. Thither the works of every family be brought into certain houses, and every kind of thing is laid up several in barns or storehouses. From hence the father of every family or every householder fetcheth whatsoever he and his have need of, and carrieth it away with him without money, without exchange, without any gage, pawn, or pledge. For why should anything be denied unto him, seeing there is abundance of all things, and that it is not to be feared lest any man will ask more than he needeth? For why should it be thought that that man would ask more than enough which is sure never to lack? Certainly in all kinds of living creatures either fear of lack doth cause covetousness and ravin, or in man only pride, which counteth it a glorious thing to pass and excel other in the superfluous and vain ostentation of things. The which kind of vice among the Utopians can have no place.

Next to the market-places that I spake of stand meat markets, whither be brought not only all sorts of herbs and the fruits of trees, with bread, but also fish, and all manner of four-footed beasts and wild fowl that be man's meat. But first the filthiness and ordure thereof is clean washed away in the running river without the city in places appointed meet for the same purpose. From thence the beasts be brought in, killed, and clean washed by the hands of their bondmen. For they permit not their free citizens to accustom themselves to the killing of beasts, through the use whereof they think clemency, the gentlest affection of our nature, by little and little to decay and perish. Neither they suffer anything that is filthy, loathsome, or uncleanly to be brought into the city, lest the air, by the stench thereof infected and corrupt, should cause pestilent diseases.

Moreover, every street hath certain great large halls set in equal distance one from another, every one known by a several name. In these halls dwell the Syphogrants, and to every one of the same halls be appointed thirty families, on either side fifteen. The stewards of every hall at a certain hour come in to the meat markets, where they receive meat according to the number of their halls. But first and chiefly of all, respect is had to the sick that be cured in the hospitals. For in the circuit of the city, a little without the walls, they have four hospitals, so big, so wide, so ample, and so large, that they may seem four little towns, which were devised of that bigness partly to the intent the sick, be they never so many in number, should not lie too throng or strait, and therefore uneasily and incommodiously; and partly that they which were taken and holden with contagious diseases, such as be wont by infection to creep from one to another, might be laid apart far from the company of the residue. These hospitals be so well appointed, and with all things necessary to health so furnished, and, moreover, so diligent attendance through the continual presence of cunning physicians is given, that though no man be sent thither against his will, yet notwithstanding there is no sick person in all the city that had not rather lie there than at home in his own house. When the steward of the sick hath received such meat as the physicians have prescribed, then the best is equally divided among the halls, according to the company of every one, saving that there is had a respect to the prince, the bishop, the Tranibores, and to ambassadors and all strangers, if there be any, which be very few and seldom. But they also, when they be there, have certain several houses appointed and prepared for them. To these halls at the set hours of dinner and supper cometh all the whole Syphogranty or ward, warned by the noise of a brazen trumpet, except such as be sick in the hospitals, or else in their own houses. Howbeit, no man is prohibited or forbid, after the halls be served, to fetch home meat out of the market to his own house, for they know that no man will do it without a cause reasonable. For though no man be prohibited to dine at home, yet no man doth it willingly because it is counted a point of small honesty. And also it were a folly to take the pain to dress a bad dinner at home, when they may be welcome to good and fine fare so nigh hand at the hall.

In this hall all vile service, all slavery and drudgery, with all laboursome toil and base business, is done by bondmen. But the women of every family, by course, have the office and charge of cookery for seething and dressing the meat and ordering all things thereto belonging. They sit at three tables or more, according to the number of their company. The men sit upon the bench next the wall, and the women against them on the other side of the table, that if any sudden evil should chance to them, as many times happeneth to women with child, they may rise without trouble or disturbance of anybody, and go thence into the nursery.

The nurses sit several alone with their young sucklings in a certain parlour appointed and deputed to the same purpose, never without fire and clean water, nor yet without cradles, that when they will they may lay down the young infants, and at their pleasure take them out of their swathing clothes, and hold them to the fire, and refresh them with play. Every mother is nurse to her own child unless either death or sickness be the let. When that chanceth, the wives of the Syphogrants quickly provide a nurse; and that is not hard to be done, for they that can do it proffer themselves to no service so gladly as to that, because that there this kind of pity is much praised, and the child that is nourished ever after taketh his nurse for his own natural mother. Also among the nurses sit all the children that be under the age of five years. All the other children of both kinds as well boys as girls, that be under the age of marriage, do either serve at the tables or else, if they be too young thereto, yet they stand by with marvellous silence. That which is given to them from the table they eat, and other several dinner time they have none.

The Syphogrant and his wife sit in the midst of the high table, forasmuch as that is counted the honourablest place, and because from thence all the whole company is in their sight. For that table standeth overthwart the over end of the hall. To them be joined two of the ancientest and eldest, for at every table they sit four at a mess. But if there be a church standing in that Syphogranty or ward, then the priest and his wife sitteth with the Syphogrant, as chief in the company. On both sides of them sit young men, and next unto them again old men. And thus throughout all the house equal of age be set together, and yet be minced and matched with unequal ages. This, they say, was ordained to the intent that the sage gravity and reverence of the elders should keep the youngers from wanton licence of words and behaviour, forasmuch as nothing can be so secretly spoken or done at the table, but either they that sit on the one side or on the other must needs perceive it. The dishes be not set down in order from the first place, but all the old men (whose places be marked with some special token to be known) be first served of their meat, and then the residue equally. The old men divide their dainties as they think best to the younger on each side of them. Thus the elders be not defrauded of their due honour, and nevertheless equal commodity cometh to every one.

They begin every dinner and supper of reading something that pertaineth to good manners and virtue; but it is short, because no man shall be grieved therewith. Hereof the elders take occasion of honest communication, but neither sad nor unpleasant. Howbeit, they do not spend all the whole dinner time themselves with long and tedious talks, but they gladly hear also the young men, yea, and purposely provoke them to talk, to the intent that they may have a proof of every man's wit and towardness or disposition to virtue, which commonly in the liberty of feasting doth shew and utter itself. Their dinners be very short, but their suppers be somewhat longer, because that after dinner followeth labour, after supper sleep and natural rest, which they think to be of more strength and efficacy to wholesome and healthful digestion. No supper is passed without music, nor their banquets lack no conceits nor junkets. They burn sweet gums and spices or perfumes and pleasant smells, and sprinkle about sweet ointments and waters, yea, they leave nothing undone that maketh for the cheering of the company. For they be much inclined to this opinion, to think no kind of pleasure forbidden whereof cometh no harm. Thus, therefore, and after this sort they live together in the city; but in the country they that dwell alone far from any neighbours do dine and sup at home in their own houses. For no family there lacketh any kind of victuals, as from whom cometh all that the citizens eat and live by.

Of their Journeying or Travelling abroad, with divers other Matters cunningly Reasoned and wittily Discussed

But if any be desirous to visit either their friends dwelling in another city or to see the place itself, they easily obtain licence of their Syphogrants and Tranibores, unless there be some profitable let. No man goeth out alone, but a company is sent forth together with their prince's letters, which do testify that they have licence to go that journey and prescribeth also the day of their return. They have a wagon given them with a common bondmnn which driveth the oxen and taketh charge of them. But unless they have women in their company, they send home the wagon again as an impediment and a let. And though they carry nothing forth with them, yet in all their journey they lack nothing, for wheresoever they come they be at home. If they tarry in a place longer than one day, then there every one of them falleth to his own occupation, and be very gently entertained of the workmen and companies of the same crafts. If any man, of his own head and without leave, walk out of his precinct and bounds, taken without the prince's letters he is brought again for a fugitive or a runaway with great shame and rebuke, and is sharply punished. If he be taken in that fault again, he is punished with bondage. If any be desirous to walk abroad into the fields or into the country that belongeth to the same city that he dwelleth in, obtaining the goodwill of his father and the consent of his wife, he is not prohibited. But into what part of the country soever he cometh he hath no meat given him until he have wrought out his forenoon's task or dispatched so much work as there is wont to be wrought before supper. Observing this law and condition, he may go whither he will within the bounds of his own city; for he shall be no less profitable to the city than if he were within it. Now you see how little liberty they have to loiter, how they can have no cloak or pretence to idleness. There be neither wine-taverns, nor ale-houses, nor stews, nor any occasion of vice or wickedness, no lurking corners, no places of wicked councils or unlawful assemblies. But they be in the present sight and under the eyes of every man. So that of necessity they must either apply their accustomed labours, or else recreate themselves with honest and laudable pastimes.

This fashion and trade of life being used among the people, it cannot be chosen but that they must of necessity have store and plenty of all things. And seeing they be all thereof partners equally, therefore can no man there be poor or needy. In the council of Amaurote, whither, as I said, every city sendeth three men apiece yearly, as soon as it is perfectly known of what things there is in every place plenty, and again what things be scant in any place, incontinent the lack of the one is performed and filled up with the abundance of the other. And this they do freely without any benefit, taking nothing again of them to whom the thing is given, but those cities that have given of their store to any other city that lacketh, requiring nothing again of the same city, do take such things as they lack of another city to the which they gave nothing. So the whole island is as it were one family or household. But when they have made sufficient provision of store for themselves (which they think not done until they have provided for two years following, because of the uncertainty of the next year's proof), then of those things whereof they have abundance they carry forth into other countries great plenty: as grain, honey, wool, flax, wood, madder, purple-dyed fells, wax, tallow, leather, and living beasts. And the seventh part of all these things they give frankly and freely to the poor of that country. The residue they sell at a reasonable and mean price. By this trade of traffic or merchandise they bring into their own country not only great plenty of gold and silver, but also all such things as they lack at home, which is almost nothing but iron. And by reason they have long used this trade, now they have more abundance of these things than any men will believe.

Now, therefore, they care not whether they sell for ready money, or else upon trust to be paid at a day and to have the most part in debts. But in so doing they never follow the credence of private men, but the assurance or warrantise of the whole city by instruments and writings made in that behalf accordingly. When the day of payment is come and expired, the city gathereth up the debt of the private debtors and putteth it into the common box, and so long hath the use and profit of it until the Utopians, their creditors, demand it. The most part of it they never ask, for that thing which is to them no profit to take it from other to whom it is profitable, they think it no right nor conscience. But if the case so stand that they must lend part of that money to another people, then they require their debt, or when they have war. For the which purpose only they keep at home all the treasure which they have, to be helpen and succoured by it either in extreme jeopardies, or in sudden dangers, but especially and chiefly to hire therewith, and that for unreasonable great wages, strange soldiers. For they had rather put strangers in jeopardy than their own country-men, knowing that for money enough their enemies themselves many times may be bought or sold, or else through treason be set together by the ears among themselves. For this cause they keep an inestimable treasure, but yet not as a treasure, but so they have it and use it, as in good faith I am ashamed to shew, fearing that my words shall not be believed. And this I have more cause to fear, for that I know how difficult and hardly I myself would have believed another man telling the same, if I had not presently seen it with mine own eyes.

For it must needs be that how far a thing is dissonant and disagreeing from the guise and trade of the hearers, so far shall it be out of their belief. Howbeit, a wise and indifferent esteemer of things will not greatly marvel perchance, seeing all their other laws and customs do so much differ from ours, if the use also of gold and silver among them be applied rather to their own fashions than to ours. I mean, in that they occupy not money them-selves, but keep it for that chance which, as it may happen, so it may be that it shall never come to pass. In the meantime gold and silver, whereof money is made, they do so use as none of them doth more esteem it than the very nature of the thing deserveth. And then who doth not plainly see how far it is under iron, as without the which men can no better live than without fire and water? Whereas to gold and silver nature hath given no use that we may not well lack if that the folly of men had not set it in higher estimation for the rareness' sake. But of the contrary part, nature, as a most tender and loving mother, hath placed the best and most necessary things open abroad, as the air, the water, and the earth itself, and hath removed and hid farthest from us vain and unprofitable things. Therefore if these metals among them should be fast locked up in some tower, it might be suspected that the prince and the council (as the people is ever foolishly imagining) intended by some subtlety to deceive the commons and to take some profit of it to themselves. Furthermore, if they should make thereof plate and such other finely and cunningly wrought stuff, if at any time they should have occasion to break it and melt it again, therewith to pay their soldiers' wages, they see and perceive very well that men would be loath to part from those things, that they once began to have pleasure and delight in. To remedy all this they have found out a means which, as it is agreeable to all their other laws and customs, so it is from ours (where gold is so much set by and so diligently kept) very far discrepant and repugnant, and therefore incredible, but only to them 33 that be wise. For whereas they eat and drink in earthen and glass vessels which, indeed, be curiously and properly made and yet be of very small value, of gold and silver they make commonly chamber-pots and other vessels that serve for most vile uses not only in their common halls but in every man's private house. Furthermore, of the same metals they make great chains, fetters, and gyves wherein they tie their bondmen. Finally whosoever for any offence be infamed, by their ears hang rings of gold, upon their fingers they wear rings of gold, and about their necks chains of gold, and, in conclusion, their heads be tied about with gold. Thus by all means possible they procure to have gold and silver among them in reproach and infamy. And these metals, which other nations do as grievously and sorrowfully forgo, as in a manner their own lives, if they should altogether at once be taken from the Utopians, no man there would think that he had lost the worth of one farthing. They gather also pearls by the seaside, and diamonds and carbuncles upon certain rocks; and yet they seek not for them, but by chance finding them, they cut and polish them, and therewith they deck their young infants. Which, like as in the first years of their childhood they make much and be fond and proud of such ornaments, so when they be a little more grown in years and discretion, perceiving that none but children do wear such toys and trifles, they lay them away even of their own shamefastness, without any bidding of their

parents, even as our children, when they wax big, do cast

away nuts, brooches, and puppets. Therefore these laws and customs, which be so far different from all other nations, how divers fantasies also and minds they do cause, did I never so plainly perceive as in the ambassadors of the Anemolians.

These ambassadors came to Amaurote while I was there. And because they came to entreat of great and weighty matters, those three citizens apiece out of every city were come thither before them. But all the ambassadors of the next countries, which had been there before and knew the fashions and manners of the Utopians, among whom they perceived no honour given to sumptuous apparel, silks to be condemned, gold also to be infamed and reproachful, were wont to come thither in very homely and simple array. But the Anemolians, because they dwell far thence and had very little acquaintance with them, hearing that they were all apparelled alike, and that very rudely and homely, thinking them not to have the things which they did not wear, being therefore more proud than wise, determined in the gorgeousness of their apparel to represent very gods, and with the bright shining and glistering of their gay clothing to dazzle the eyes of the silly poor Utopians. So there came in three ambassadors with an hundred servants all apparelled in changeable colours, the most of them in silks. The ambassadors themselves (for at home in their own country they were noblemen) in cloth of gold, with great chains of gold, with gold hanging at their ears, with gold rings upon their fingers, with brooches and aglets of gold upon their caps which glistered full of pearls and precious stones, to be short, trimmed and adorned with all those things which among the Utopians were either the punishment of bondmen or the reproach of infamed persons or else trifles for young children to play withal.

Therefore it would have done a man good at his heart to have seen how proudly they displayed their peacock's feathers, how much they made of their painted sheaths, and how loftily they set forth and advanced themselves when they compared their gallant apparel with the poor raiment of the Utopians. For all the people were swarmed forth into the streets. And on the other side it was no less pleasure to consider how much they were deceived and how far they missed of their purpose, being contrarywise taken than they thought they should have been. For to the eyes of all the Utopians, except very few which had been in other countries for some reasonable cause, all that gorgeousness of apparel seemed shameful and reproachful. Insomuch that they most reverently saluted the vilest and most abject of them for lords, passing over the ambassadors themselves without any honour, judging them by their wearing of golden chains to be bondmen. Yea, you should have seen children also that had cast away their pearls and precious stones, when they saw the like sticking upon the ambassadors' caps, dig and push their mothers under the sides, saying thus to them: Look, 36 mother, how great a lubber doth yet wear pearls and precious stones as though he were a little child still. But the mother, yea and that also in good earnest, Peace, son, saith she, I think he be some of the ambassadors' fools. Some found fault at their golden chains as to no use nor purpose, being so small and weak that a bondman might easily break them, and again so wide and large, that when it pleased him he might cast them off and run away at liberty whither he would. But when the ambassadors had been there a day or two and saw so great abundance of gold so lightly esteemed, yea, in no less reproach than it was with them in honour, and, besides that, more gold in the chains and gyves of one fugitive bondman than all the costly ornaments of them three was worth, they began to abate their courage, and for very shame laid away all that gorgeous array whereof they were so proud, and specially when they had talked familiarly with the Utopians, and had learned all their fashions and opinions.

For they marvel that any men be so foolish as to have delight and pleasure in the doubtful glistering of a little trifling stone, which may behold any of the stars, or else the sun itself. Or that any man is so mad as to count himself the nobler for the smaller or finer thread of wool, which self-same wool (be it now in never so fine a spun thread) a sheep did once wear, and yet was she all that time no other thing than a sheep. They marvel also that gold, which of its own nature is a thing so unprofitable, is now among all people in so high estimation, that man himself, by whom, yea, and for the use of whom, it is so much set by, is in much less estimation than the gold itself. Insomuch that a lumpish blockheaded churl, and which hath no more wit than an ass, yea, and as full of naughtiness as of folly, shall have nevertheless many wise and good men in subjection and bondage only for this, because he hath a great heap of gold. Which if it should be taken from him by any fortune or by some subtle wile and cautel of the law (which no less than fortune doth both raise up the low and pluck down the high) and be given to the most vile slave and abject drivel of all his household, then shortly after he shall go into the service of his servant, as an augmentation or overplus beside his money. But they much more marvel at and detest the madness of them which to those rich men, in whose debt and danger they be not, do give almost divine honours for none other consideration but because they be rich, and yet knowing them to be such niggish pennyfathers, that they be sure as long as they live not the worth of one farthing of that heap of gold shall come to them.

These and suchlike opinions have they conceived partly by education, being brought up in that commonwealth whose laws and customs be far different from these kinds of folly, and partly by good literature and learning. For though there be not many in every city which be exempt and discharged of all other labours and appointed only to learning (that is to say, such in whom, even from their very childhood, they have perceived a singular toward-
38 ness, a fine wit, and a mind apt to good learning), yet all

in their childhood be instruct in learning. And the better part of the people, both men and women, throughout all their whole life do bestow in learning those spare hours which we said they have vacant from bodily labours. They be taught learning in their own native tongue. For it is both copious in words and also pleasant to the ear, and for the utterance of a man's mind very perfect and sure. The most part of all that side of the world useth the same language, saving that among the Utopians it is finest and purest, and according to the diversity of the countries it is diversely altered. Of all these philosophers whose names be here famous in this part of the world to us known, before our coming thither not as much as the fame of any of them was common among them. And yet in music, logic, arithmetic, and geometry they have found out in a manner all that our ancient philosophers have taught.

But as they in all things be almost equal to our old ancient clerks, so our new logicians in subtle inventions have far passed and gone beyond them. For they have not devised one of all those rules of restrictions, amplifications, and suppositions, very wittily invented in the small logicals which here our children in every place do learn. Furthermore, they were never yet able to find out the second intentions, insomuch that none of them all could ever see man himself in common, as they call him, though he be (as you know) bigger than ever was any giant, yea, and pointed to of us even with our finger.

But they be in the course of the stars and the movings of the heavenly spheres very expert and cunning. They have also wittily excogitated and devised instruments of divers fashions, wherein is exactly comprehended and contained the movings and situations of the sun, the moon, and of all the other stars which appear in their horizon. But as for the amities and dissensions of the planets, and all that deceitful divination by the stars, they never as much as dreamed thereof. Rains, winds, and other courses of tempest they know before by certain tokens which they have learned by long use and observation. But of the causes of all these things and of the ebbing, flowing, and saltness of the sea, and finally of the original beginning and nature of heaven and of the world, they hold partly the same opinions that our old philosophers hold, and partly, as our philosophers vary among themselves, so they also, while they bring new reasons of things, do disagree from all them, and yet among themselves in all points they do not accord.

In that part of philosophy which entreateth of manners and virtue their reasons and opinions agree with ours. They dispute of the good qualities of the soul, of the body, and of fortune, and whether the name of goodness may be applied to all these or only to the endowments and gifts of the soul. They reason of virtue and pleasure; but the chief and principal question is in what thing, be it one or more, the felicity of man consisteth. But in this point they seem almost too much given and inclined to the opinion of them which defend pleasure, wherein they determine either all or the chiefest part of man's felicity to rest. And (which is more to be marvelled at) the defence of this so dainty and delicate an opinion they fetch even from their grave, sharp, bitter, and rigorous religion. For they never dispute of felicity or blessedness but they join unto the reasons of philosophy certain principles taken out of religion, without the which to the investigation of true felicity they think reason of itself weak and unperfect. Those principles be these and such-like: That the soul is immortal, and by the bountiful goodness of God ordained to felicity. That to our virtues and good deeds rewards be appointed after this life, and to our evil deeds punishments. Though these be pertaining to religion, yet they think it meet that they should be believed and granted by proofs of reason. But if these principles were condemned and disannulled, then without any delay they pronounce no man to be so foolish which would not do all his diligence and endeavour to obtain pleasure by right or wrong, only avoiding this inconvenience, that the less pleasure should not be a let or hindrance to the bigger, or that he laboured not for that pleasure which would bring after it displeasure, grief, and sorrow. For they judge it extreme madness to follow sharp and painful virtue, and not only to banish the pleasure of life, but also willingly to suffer grief, without any hope of profit thereof ensuing. For what profit can there be if a man, when he hath passed over all his life unpleasantly, that is to say, miserably, shall have no, reward after his death?

But now, sir, they think not felicity to rest in all pleasure, but only in that pleasure that is good and honest, and that hereto as to perfect blessedness our nature is allured and drawn even of virtue, whereto only they that be of the contrary opinion do attribute felicity. For they define virtue to be life ordered according to nature, and that we be hereunto ordained of God. And that he doth follow the course of nature, which in desiring and refusing things is ruled by reason. Furthermore, that reason doth chiefly and principally kindle in men the love and veneration of the Divine Majesty of whose goodness it is that we be, and that we be in possibility to attain felicity. And that secondarily it both stirreth and provoketh us to lead our life out of care in joy and mirth, and also moveth us to help and further all other in respect of the society of nature to obtain and enjoy the same.

For there was never man so earnest and painful a follower of virtue and hater of pleasure, that would so enjoin you labours, watchings, and fastings, but he would also exhort you to ease, lighten, and relieve, to your power, the lack and misery of others, praising the same as a deed of humanity and pity. Then, if it be a point of humanity for man to bring health and comfort to man, and specially (which is a virtue most peculiarly belonging to man) to mitigate and assuage the grief of others, and by taking from them the sorrow and heaviness of life to restore them to joy, that is to say, to pleasure, why may it not then be said that nature doth provoke every man to do the same to himself? For a joyful life, that is to say, a pleasant life, is either evil; and if it be so, then thou shouldest not only help no man thereto, but rather, as much as in thee lieth, withdraw all men from it as noisome and hurtful; or else if thou not only mayst, but also of duty art bound, to procure it to other, why not chiefly to thyself to whom thou art bound to shew as much favour and gentleness as to other? For when nature biddeth thee to be good and gentle to other she commandeth thee not to be cruel and ungentle to thyself. Therefore even very nature (say they) prescribeth to us a joyful life, that is to say, pleasure, as the end of all our operations. And they define virtue to be life ordered according to the prescript of nature.

But in that that nature doth allure and provoke men one to help another to live merrily (which surely she doth not without a good cause, for no man is so far above the lot of man's state or condition, that nature doth cark and care for him only which equally favoureth all that be comprehended under the communion of one shape, form, and fashion), verily she commandeth thee to use diligent circumspection, that thou do not so seek for thine own commodities, that thou procure others' incommodities. Wherefore their opinion is, that not only covenants and bargains made among private men ought to be well and faithfully fulfilled, observed, and kept, but also common laws, which either a good prince hath justly published, or else the people, neither oppressed with tyranny, neither deceived by fraud and guile, hath by their common consent constituted and ratified concerning the partition of the commodities of life, that is to say, the matter of pleasure. These laws not offended, it is wisdom that thou look to thine own wealth. And to do the same for the commonwealth is no less than thy duty, if thou bearest any reverent love or any natural zeal and affection to thy native country. But to go about to let another man of his pleasure whiles thou procurest thine own, that is open wrong. Contrariwise, to withdraw something from thyself to give to others, that is a point of humanity and gentleness, which never taketh away so much commodity as it bringeth again. For it is recompensed with the return of benefits; and the conscience of the good deed, with the remembrance of the thankful love and benevolence of them to whom thou hast done it, doth bring more pleasure to thy mind than that which thou hast withholden from thyself could have brought to thy body. Finally (which to a godly-disposed and a religious mind is easy to be persuaded), God recompenseth the gift of a short and small pleasure with great and everlasting joy.

Therefore, the matter diligently weighed and considered, thus they think, that all our actions, and in them the virtues themselves, be referred at the last to pleasure as their end and felicity. Pleasure they call every motion

and state of the body or mind wherein man hath naturally

delectation. Appetite they join to nature, and that not without a good cause. For like as not only the senses, but also right reason, coveteth whatsoever is naturally pleasant, so that it may be gotten without wrong or injury, not letting or debarring a greater pleasure nor causing painful labour, even so those things that men by vain imagination do feign against nature to be pleasant (as though it lay in their power to change the things, as they do the names of things), all such pleasures they believe to be of so small help and furtherance to felicity, that they count them a great let and hindrance. Because that in whom they have once taken place, all his mind they possess with a false opinion of pleasure, so that there is no place left for true and natural delectations. For there be many things which of their own nature contain no pleasantness, yea, the most part of them much grief and sorrow; and yet, through the perverse and malicious flickering enticements of lewd and unhonest desires, be taken not only for special and sovereign pleasures, but also be counted among the chief causes of life.

In this counterfeit kind of pleasure they put them that I spake of before, which, the better gowns they have on, the better men they think themselves. In the which thing they do twice err, for they be no less deceived in that they think their gown the better, than they be in that they think themselves the better. For if you consider the profitable use of the garment, why should wool of a finer-spun thread be thought better than the wool of a coarse-spun thread? Yet they, as though the one did pass the other by nature and not by their mistaking, advance themselves, and think the price of their own persons thereby greatly increased. And therefore the honour which in a coarse gown they durst not have looked for, they require, as it were of duty, for their finer gown's sake. And if they be passed by without reverence, they take it displeasantly and disdainfully. And again, is it not like madness to take a pride in vain and unprofitable honours? For what natural or true pleasure dost thou take of another man's bare head or bowed knees? Will this ease the pain of thy knees or remedy the frenzy of thy head? In this image of counterfeit pleasure they be of a marvellous madness, which for the opinion of nobility rejoice much in their own conceit, because it was their fortune to come of such ancestors whose stock of long time hath been counted rich (for now nobility is nothing else), specially rich in lands. And though their ancestors left them not one foot of land, or else they themselves have pissed it against the walls, yet they think themselves not the less noble therefore of one hair.

In this number also they count them that take pleasure and delight (as I said) in gems and precious stones, and think themselves almost gods if they chance to get an excellent one, specially of that kind which in that time of their own countrymen is had in highest estimation. For one kind of stone keepeth not his price still in all countries and at all times. Nor they buy them not, but taken out of the gold and bare; no nor so neither, until they have made the seller to swear that he will warrant and assure it to be a true stone and no counterfeit gem. Such care they take lest a counterfeit stone should deceive their eyes instead of a right stone. But why shouldest thou not take even as much pleasure in beholding a counterfeit stone, which thine eye cannot discern from a right stone? They should both be of like value to thee, even as to the blind man. What shall I say of them that keep superfluous riches, to take delectation only in the beholding and not in the use or occupying thereof? Do they take true pleasure, or else be they deceived with false pleasure? Or of them that be in a contrary vice, hiding the gold which they shall never occupy, nor peradventure never see more? And whiles they take care lest they shall lose it, do lose it indeed. For what is it else when they hide it in the ground, taking it both from their own use and perchance from all other men's also? And yet thou, when thou hast hid thy treasure, as one out of all care hoppest for joy. The which treasure, if it should chance to be stolen, and thou ignorant of the theft shouldst die ten years after, all that ten years' space that thou livest after thy money was stolen, what matter was it to thee whether it had been taken away or else safe as thou leftest it? Truly both ways like profit came to thee.

To these so foolish pleasures they join dicers, whose madness they know by hearsay and not by use. Hunters also, and hawkers. For what pleasure is there (say they) in casting the dice upon a table, which thou hast done so often, that if there were any pleasure in it, yet the oft use might make thee weary thereof? Or what delight can there be, and not rather displeasure, in hearing the barking and howling of dogs? Or what greater pleasure is there to be felt when a dog followeth an hare than when a dog followeth a dog? For one thing is done in both, that is to say, running, if thou hast pleasure therein. But if the hope of slaughter and the expectation of tearing in pieces the beast doth please thee, thou shouldest rather be moved with pity to see a silly innocent hare murdered of a dog: the weak of the stronger, the fearful of the fierce, the innocent of the cruel and unmerciful. Therefore all this exercise of hunting, as a thing unworthy to be used of free men, the Utopians have rejected to their butchers, to the which craft (as we said before) they appoint their bondmen. For they count hunting the lowest, the vilest, and most abject part of butchery, and the other parts of it more profitable and more honest, as bringing much more commodity, in that they kill beasts only for necessity, whereas the hunter seeketh nothing but pleasure of the silly and woeful beast's slaughter and murder. The which pleasure in beholding death they think doth rise in the very beasts, either of a cruel affection of mind, or else to be changed in continuance of time into cruelty by long use of so cruel a pleasure.

These, therefore, and all suchlike, which be innumerable, though the common sort of people doth take them

for pleasures, yet they, seeing there is no natural pleasant-ness in them, do plainly determine them to have no affinity with true and right pleasure. For as touching that they do commonly move the sense with delectation (which seemeth to be a work of pleasure), this doth nothing diminish their opinion. For not the nature of the thing, but their perverse and lewd custom is the cause hereof, which causeth them to accept bitter or sour things for sweet things even as women with child in their vitiate and corrupt taste think pitch and tallow sweeter than any honey. Howbeit, no man's judgment depraved and cor-rupt, either by sickness or by custom, can change the nature of pleasure more than it can do the nature of other things.

They make divers kinds of true pleasures. For some they attribute to the soul and some to the body. To the soul they give intelligence and that delectation that cometh of the contemplation of truth. Hereunto is joined the pleasant remembrance of the good life past. The pleasure of the body they divide into two parts. The first is when delectation is sensibly felt and perceived, which many times chanceth by the renewing and refreshing of those parts which our natural heat drieth up. This cometh by meat and drink, and sometimes whiles those things be expulsed and voided, whereof is in the body over-great abundance. This pleasure is felt when we do our natural easement, or when we be doing the act of generation, or when the itching of any part is eased with rubbing or 49 scratching. Sometimes pleasure riseth exhibiting to any member nothing that it desireth, nor taking from it any pain that it feeleth, which nevertheless tickleth and moveth our senses with a certain secret efficacy, but with a manifest motion turneth them to it; as is that which cometh of music. The second part of bodily pleasure, they say, is that which consisteth and resteth in the quiet and upright state of the body. And that truly is every man's own proper health, intermingled and disturbed with no grief. For this, if it be not letted nor assaulted with no grief, is delectable of itself, though it be moved with no external or outward pleasure. For though it be not so plain and manifest to the sense as the greedy lust of eating and drinking, yet, nevertheless, many take it for the chiefest pleasure. All the Utopians grant it to be a right sovereign pleasure and, as you would say, the foundation and ground of all pleasures, as which even alone is able to make the state and condition of life delectable and pleasant; and it being once taken away, there is no place left for any pleasure. For to be without grief not having health, that they call insensibility and not pleasure.

The Utopians have long ago rejected and condemned the opinion of them which said that steadfast and quiet health (for this question also hath been diligently debated among them) ought not therefore to be counted a pleasure, because, they say, it cannot be presently and sensibly perceived and felt by some outward motion. But of the contrary part now they agree almost all in this, that health is a most sovereign pleasure. For seeing that in sickness (say they) is grief, which is a mortal enemy to pleasure, even as sickness is to health, why should not then pleasure be in the quietness of health? For they say it maketh nothing to this matter, whether you say that sickness is a grief, or that in sickness is grief, for all cometh to one purpose. For whether health be a pleasure itself, or a necessary cause of pleasure, as fire is of heat, truly both ways it followeth that they cannot be without pleasure that be in perfect health. Furthermore, whiles we eat (say they), then health, which began to be appaired, fighteth by the help of food against hunger. In the which fight, whiles health by little and little getteth the upper hand, that same proceeding and (as ye would say) that onwardness to the wont strength ministreth that pleasure whereby we be so refreshed. Health, therefore, which in the conflict is joyful, shall it not be merry when it hath gotten the victory? But as soon as it hath recovered the pristinate strength, which thing only in all the fight it coveted, shall it incontinent be astonied? Nor shall it not know nor embrace the own wealth and goodness? For where it is said health cannot be felt, this, they think, is nothing true. For what man waking, say they, feeleth not himself in health, but he that is not? Is there any man so possessed with stonish insensibility or with lethargy, that is to say, the sleeping sickness, that he will not grant health to be acceptable to him, and delectable?

But what other thing is delectation than that which by another name is called pleasure? They embrace chiefly the pleasures of the mind, for them they count the chiefest and most principal of all. The chief part of them they think doth come of the exercise of virtue and conscience of good life. Of these pleasures that the body ministreth, they give the pre-eminence to health. For the delight of eating and drinking, and whatsoever hath any like pleasantness, they determine to be pleasures much to be desired, but no other ways than for health's sake. For such things of their own proper nature be not so pleasant, but in that they resist sickness privily stealing on. Therefore, like as it is a wise man's part rather to avoid sickness than to wish for medicines, and rather to drive away and put to flight careful griefs than to call for comfort, so it is much better not to need this kind of pleasure than thereby to be eased of the contrary grief. The which kind of pleasure if any man take for his felicity, that man must needs grant that then he shall be in most felicity, if he live that life which is led in continual hunger, thirst, itching, eating, drinking, scratching, and rubbing. The which life how not only foul and unhonest, but also how miserable and wretched it is, who perceiveth not? These doubtless be the basest pleasures of all, as unpure and unperfect. For they never come, but accompanied with their contrary griefs, as with the pleasure of eating is joined hunger, and that after no very equal sort. For of these

two the grief is both the more vehement and also of

longer continuance, for it beginneth before the pleasure, and endeth not until the pleasure die with it.

Wherefore such pleasures they think not greatly to be set by, but in that they be necessary. Howbeit, they have delight also in these, and thankfully knowledge the tender love of mother nature, which with most pleasant delectation allureth her children to that, to the necessary use whereof they must from time to time continually be forced and driven. For how wretched and miserable should our life be, if these daily griefs of hunger and thirst could not be driven away but with bitter potions and sour medicines, as the other diseases be wherewith we be seldomer troubled? But beauty, strength, nimbleness, these as peculiar and pleasant gifts of nature they make much of. But those pleasures that be received by the ears, the eyes, and the nose, which nature willeth to be proper and peculiar to man (for no other living creature doth behold the fairness and the beauty of the world or is moved with any respect of savours, but only for the diversity of meats, neither perceiveth the concordant and discordant distances of sounds and tunes), these pleasures, I say, they accept and allow as certain pleasant rejoicings of life. But in all things this cautel they use, that a less pleasure hinder not a bigger, and that the pleasure be no cause of displeasure, which they think to follow of necessity if the pleasure be unhonest. But yet to despise the comeliness of beauty, to waste the bodily strength, to turn nimbleness into sluggishness, to consume and make feeble the body with fasting, to do injury to health, and to reject the pleasant motions of nature (unless a man neglect these commodities whiles he doth with a fervent zeal procure the wealth of others or the common profit, for the which pleasure forborne he is in hope of a greater pleasure at God's hand), else for a vain shadow of virtue for the wealth and profit of no man, to punish himself, or to the intent he may be able courageously to suffer adversity (which perchance shall never come to him), this to do they think it a point of extreme madness, and a token of a man cruelly minded towards himself and unkind towards nature, as one so disdaining to be in her danger, that he renounceth and refuseth all her benefits.

This is their sentence and opinion of virtue and pleasure, and they believe that by man's reason none can be found truer than this, unless any godlier be inspired into man from heaven. Wherein whether they believe well or no, neither the time doth suffer us to discuss, neither it is now necessary. For we have taken upon us to shew and declare their laws and ordinances, and not to defend them. But this thing I believe verily: howsoever these decrees be, that there is in no place of the world neither a more excellent people, neither a more flourishing commonwealth. They be light and quick of body, full of activity and nimbleness, and of more strength than a man would judge them by their stature, which for all that is not too low. And though their soil be not very fruitful, nor their air very wholesome, yet against the air they so defend them with temperate diet, and so order and husband their ground with diligent travail, that in no country is greater increase and plenty of corn and cattle, nor men's bodies of longer life and subject or apt to fewer diseases. There, therefore, a man may see well and diligently exploited and furnished, not only those things which husbandmen do commonly in other countries, as by craft and cunning to remedy the barrenness of the ground, but also a whole wood by the hands of the people plucked up by the roots in one place, and set again in another place. Wherein was had regard and consideration, not of plenty, but of commodious carriage, that wood and timber might be nigher to the sea or the rivers or the cities; for it is less labour and business to carry grain far by land than wood. The people be gentle, merry, quick, and fine witted, delighting in quietness and, when need requireth, able to abide and suffer much bodily labour. Else they be not greatly desirous and fond of it; but in the exercise and study of the mind they be never weary.

When they had heard me speak of the Greek literature or learning (for in Latin there was nothing that I thought they would greatly allow, besides historians and poets) they made wonderful earnest and importunate suit unto me that I would teach and instruct them in that tongue and learning. I began, therefore, to read unto them at the first, truly, more because I would not seem to refuse the 55 labour than that I hoped that they would anything profit therein. But when I had gone forward a little, I perceived incontinent by their diligence that my labour should not be bestowed in vain. For they began so easily to fashion their letters, so plainly to pronounce the words, so quickly to learn by heart, and so surely to rehearse the same, that I marvelled at it, saving that the most part of them were fine and chosen wits, and of ripe age, picked out of the company of the learned men which not only of their own free and voluntary will, but also by the commandment of the council, undertook to learn this language. Therefore in less than three years' space there was nothing in the Greek tongue that they lacked. They were able to read good authors without any stay, if the book were not false. This kind of learning, as I suppose, they took so much the sooner because, it is somewhat alliant to them. For I think that this nation took their beginning of the Greeks, because their speech, which in all other points is not much unlike the Persian tongue, keepeth divers signs and tokens of the Greek language in the names of their cities and of their magistrates.

They have of me (for when I was determined to enter into my fourth voyage, I cast into the ship in the stead of merchandise a pretty fardel of books, because I intended to come again rather never than shortly), they have, I say, of me the most part of Plato's works, more of Aristotle's, also Theophrastus of plants, but in divers places (which I am sorry for) unperfect. For whiles we were a-shipboard a marmoset chanced upon the book as it was negligently laid by, which wantonly playing therewith plucked out certain leaves and tore them in pieces. Of them that have written the grammar, they have only Lascaris, for Theodorus I carried not with me, nor never a dictionary but Hesychius and Dioscorides. They set great store by Plutarch's books, and they be delighted with Lucian's merry conceits and jests. Of the poets they have Aristophanes, Homer, Euripides, and Sophocles in Aldus' small print. Of the historians they have Thucydides, Herodotus, and Herodian. Also, my companion Tricius Apinatus carried with him physic books, certain small works of Hippocrates, and Galen's *Microtechne*. The which book they have in great estimation; for though there be almost no nation under heaven that hath less need of physic than they, yet this notwithstanding, physic is nowhere in greater honour, because they count the knowledge of it among the goodliest and most profitable parts of philosophy. For whiles they by the help of this philosophy search out the secret mysteries of nature, they think themselves to receive thereby not only wonderful great pleasure, but also to obtain great thanks and favour of the Author and Maker thereof. Whom they think, according to the fashion of other artificers, to have set forth the marvellous and gorgeous frame of the world for man with great affection intentively to behold. Whom only He hath made of wit and capacity to consider and understand the excellency of so great a work. And therefore

He beareth (say they) more goodwill and love to the curious and diligent beholder and viewer of His work and marveller at the same than He doth to him which, like a very brute beast without wit and reason, or as one without sense or moving, hath no regard to so great and so wonderful a spectacle. The wits, therefore, of the Utopians, inured and exercised in learning, be marvellous quick in the invention of feats helping anything to the advantage and wealth of life. Howbeit, two feats they may thank us for, that is, the science of imprinting and the craft of making paper. And yet not only us, but chiefly and principally themselves.

For when we shewed to them Aldus his print in books of paper, and told them of the stuff whereof paper is made, and of the feat of graving letters, speaking somewhat more than we could plainly declare (for there was none of us that knew perfectly either the one or the other), they forthwith very wittily conjectured the thing. And whereas before they wrote only in skins, in barks of trees, and in reeds, now they have attempted to make paper and to imprint letters. And though at the first it proved not all of the best, yet by often assaying the same they shortly got the feat of both, and have so brought the matter about that if they had copies of Greek authors they could lack no books. But now they have no more than I rehearsed before, saving that by printing of books they have multiplied and increased the same into many thousands of copies. Whosoever cometh thither to see the land, being excellent in any gift of wit, or through much and long journeying well experienced and seen in the knowledge of many countries (for the which cause we were very welcome to them), him they receive and entertain wondrous gently and lovingly. For they have delight to hear what is done in every land, howbeit very few merchant men come thither. For what should they bring thither, unless it were iron, or else gold and silver, which they had rather carry home again? Also such things as are to be carried out of their land, they think it more wisdom to carry that gear forth themselves, than that other should come thither to fetch it, to the intent they may the better know the outlands on every side of them, and keep in use the feat and knowledge of sailing.

Phoenix 60p Paperbacks

History/Biography/Travel
The Empire of Rome A.D. 98–190 *Edward Gibbon*
The Prince *Machiavelli*
The Alan Clark Diaries: Thatcher's Fall *Alan Clark*
Churchill: Embattled Hero *Andrew Roberts*
The French Revolution *E.J. Hobsbawm*
Voyage Around the Horn *Joshua Slocum*
The Great Fire of London *Samuel Pepys*
Utopia *Thomas More*
The Holocaust *Paul Johnson*
Tolstoy and History *Isaiah Berlin*

Science and Philosophy
A Guide to Happiness *Epicurus*
Natural Selection *Charles Darwin*
Science, Mind & Cosmos *John Brockman, ed.*
Zarathustra *Friedrich Nietzsche*
God's Utility Function *Richard Dawkins*
Human Origins *Richard Leakey*
Sophie's World: The Greek Philosophers *Jostein Gaarder*
The Rights of Woman *Mary Wollstonecraft*
The Communist Manifesto *Karl Marx & Friedrich Engels*
Birds of Heaven *Ben Okri*

Fiction
Riot at Misri Mandi *Vikram Seth*
The Time Machine *H. G. Wells*
Love in the Night *F. Scott Fitzgerald*

The Murders in the Rue Morgue *Edgar Allen Poe*
The Necklace *Guy de Maupassant*
You Touched Me *D. H. Lawrence*
The Mabinogion *Anon*
Mowgli's Brothers *Rudyard Kipling*
Shancarrig *Maeve Binchy*
A Voyage to Lilliput *Jonathan Swift*

POETRY

Songs of Innocence and Experience *William Blake*
The Eve of Saint Agnes *John Keats*
High Waving Heather *The Brontes*
Sailing to Byzantium *W. B. Yeats*
I Sing the Body Electric *Walt Whitman*
The Ancient Mariner *Samuel Taylor Coleridge*
Intimations of Immortality *William Wordsworth*
Palgrave's Golden Treasury of Love Poems *Francis Palgrave*
Goblin Market *Christina Rossetti*
Fern Hill *Dylan Thomas*

LITERATURE OF PASSION

Don Juan *Lord Byron*
From Bed to Bed *Catullus*
Satyricon *Petronius*
Love Poems *John Donne*
Portrait of a Marriage *Nigel Nicolson*
The Ballad of Reading Gaol *Oscar Wilde*
Love Sonnets *William Shakespeare*
Fanny Hill *John Cleland*
The Sexual Labyrinth (for women) *Alina Reyes*
Close Encounters (for men) *Alina Reyes*